CHRISTMAS
STORIES

CHRISTMAS STORIES

Written and Illustrated by

DON CONROY

POOLBEG
FOR CHILDREN

Published 2001
by Poolbeg Press Ltd
123 Grange Hill, Baldoyle
Dublin 13, Ireland
E-mail: poolbeg@poolbeg.com
www.poolbeg.com

1 3 5 7 9 10 8 6 4 2

A catalogue record for this book is available from the British Library.

ISBN 1 84223 097 2

Cover design by Steven Hope
Illustrations by Don Conroy
Typeset by Patricia Hope in Times 16/24
Printed by The Guernsey Press Ltd,
Vale, Guernsey, Channel Islands.

About the Author

Don Conroy is Ireland's best-loved illustrator and writer for children. He is also a television personality and an enthusiastic observer of wildlife.

Also by Don Conroy

Wildlife Colouring Book
The Fox's Tale
What The Owl Saw
The Vampire Journal
The Anaconda from Drumcondra
The Elephant At The Door
The Bookworm Who Turned Over A New Leaf
Rocky The Dinosaur
Seal Of Approval
Cartoon Crazy
Rocky's Fun Book
Vampire of St Michan's

For Aindriú and Sarah

The Tree That Discovered Christmas

In a secret forest beyond Eagle Mountain lived Sappy the Conifer Tree. Broc Forest was a very large and beautiful forest. Sappy had lots of friends there: squirrels, deer, rabbits, foxes, badgers, owls, hawks, jays, woodcock, robins, blackbirds, blue tits and many more. They would all come to visit Sappy at times; the badgers would pass by most evenings to forage for grubs or worms; the fox often slept close by under the beech-tree's roots; the deer carefully picked their way through the forest and sometimes used Sappy's thin trunk as a scratching post. Sappy didn't mind; in fact it tickled him and made him laugh, especially when the big male red deer rubbed his velvet antlers up and down his trunk and along his lower branches.

Of course the squirrels were always jumping on him and eating his cones. Sappy enjoyed their crazy antics as they ran along the branches and leaped from one tree to the other. Sometimes when they knocked down the cones a woodmouse would come and nibble on them.

Yes, Sappy had lots of friends in Broc Forest. But his closest and dearest friend was Wizen the Oak Tree. Wizen was the oldest tree in the forest, with his big strong branches that seemed to reach to the sky

and his massive trunk whose girth was wider than any other forest tree. There was Eland the Copper Beech, whose bark was so smooth that the butterflies would often rest on his trunk. And in the evening the moths did the same. Then there was Brittle the Lime Tree who had bats nesting in a small hollow near the top of her trunk. Sappy would watch the long-eared bats leave their secret hiding place at dusk and go flitting away among the branches.

Sappy loved to see and listen to the woodcock go 'roding' over the tops of the trees during the breeding season. In the daytime, when this bird slept on the forest floor among the dry leaves, it was very hard to spot. On nights when there was a full moon the tawny owl would call from a nearby branch.

Of course, Sappy wasn't the only conifer in the woods. There were Scots pine and Corsican spruce too. There was even a yew tree that some said was as old as Wizen. Sappy was almost seven seasons old – there were saplings much smaller than he was and of course many much older and taller too.

Sappy loved living in the forest and seeing the seasons unfold. In winter, when the snow came and weighed heavily on his branches, Sappy would try to identify the tracks made by the animals on the snow-covered forest floor. Sometimes small bands of birds would come around and search his branches for anything to eat. Long-tailed tits, goldfinches and goldcrests would take turns to search for food. Mistle and song thrushes would be joined by their winter cousins the redwing and fieldfare.

They would visit the yew and the holly tree for berries. They were never disappointed. They even knew where the mistletoe grew. Vicky the Holly was always generous with her bounty of red berries. Sometimes the mistle thrush would break into song, especially after a storm. The song thrush too would sing a beautiful song, then when it was finished would give a repeat performance. Wizen the Oak said that the young birds had to learn how to sing from their parents.

Wizen knew all the different songs and

calls of the birds. He would often say, "There's a blackcap nearby!" or "Listen! A nightingale is approaching!" and sure enough a nightingale would come flying up the glade and alight in a thicket.

Wizen would point out to Sappy the flowers that appeared at different times of the year: the snowdrops, the primroses, later the daffodils, the woodbine, the ragged-robin and the bluebells. The old oak seemed to know about every single thing that grew or was born in the forest, and where all the different wildfolk lived: the badgers' sett, the squirrels' drey, the foxes' den and the otters' holt by the river.

All the wildfolk respected the wise old oak. They would come to Wizen for advice or to show off their new families. But the favourite time for all the wildfolk was when Wizen told his stories. The tawny

owl would inform the rest of the forest that old Wizen was about to regale them with an exciting story. Some stories were tall stories, others very funny; there were very sad stories steeped in history, and stories to ponder over, scary ones that made one afraid to go to sleep, stories that made one feel proud and strong and others that made one feel humble. Yes, Wizen was a gifted storyteller.

Late one autumn night Wizen told a story that was more of a warning tale. All the animals had gathered around the oak tree while the birds sat on his many branches.

Trees and bushes dared not rustle in case they missed anything. The trees out of range would rely on the Branch Express. This was where the story could pass from each tree through its branches, branchlets, twigs and leaves to be received by the other trees, bushes, flowers and undergrowth that were far away. It was a form of communication that only trees and plant life knew of.

Wizen stood solemnly and spoke of a terrible storm that had torn through the forests many moons ago, long before most of the young trees were even saplings. He explained how it cut through the forest uprooting many trees and sending older ones crashing to the ground. He told how he lost a dear friend, a giant walnut tree, to the violent storm, and how he accidentally pulled down other trees that were growing nearby. Several days after, men came with their axes and saws and cut the fallen trees into large, long shapes that were then hauled away by a big truck. This was during the month of March, he added.

The trees and animals gave a sigh of relief for it was late autumn and most of the nestlings had fledged and grown strong and healthy thanks to the bounty of the trees and bushes. It was the same for the young animals born in April or May. Most of them were well able to look after themselves by now.

"Well, we haven't had a storm like that for a very long time," said Eland the Copper Beech brightly.

"True," said Wizen as he looked around at all the little wildfolk and his tree families dressed in their golden autumnal colours. Then he said gravely, "I fear there is a powerful and deadly storm on the way."

The animals and birds trembled with fear. Some trees shook so much that their leaves dropped to the ground.

"When will this happen?" Sappy asked the wise old tree.

"Soon," said Wizen. "That's all I can say: soon. Very soon. I feel it coming."

Some of the trees spoke among themselves. "Perhaps old Wizen is wrong, for there is not a breath of a breeze in the air." In fact it had been a beautiful summer and autumn, with very little wind or rain.

"He shouldn't be alarming the forest denizens like that," snapped a sycamore tree to a larch. "I admit his stories are very interesting, but when he starts all this prophesying it really is too much."

"I agree," said a jay that was flitting about and collecting acorns that had fallen from the great oak.

"Well, I believe him," Sappy insisted. "And if you know what's good for you, you will be prepared."

"What can a tree do," asked a hazel, "but stand strong and hope for the best?"

The animals and birds took Wizen's words of warning very seriously indeed, and they all hurried to the safety of their secret hiding places. Next day the forest was silent. There was no birdsong to brighten the day, nor sign of any creature moving about. And the following days were the same. An eerie silence existed and the only movement was the occasional leaf floating down to the forest floor.

"See, I told you," said the sycamore to the other trees. "No sign of this deadly storm, not even a breeze. I think old Wizen is losing his marbles."

"You shouldn't speak like that," said Vicky the Holly.

There was suddenly a loud squawk of alarm from the jay, the only bird that had not heeded the old oak's advice. The jay, normally so secretive, was frantically flying about calling loudly that a storm was brewing.

"Not you too," said the sycamore.

"It's true," insisted the jay. "I was down at the far end of the forest when I saw it pushing its way over the heath, with such force that the clouds are on the run across the sky. It's going to hit the forest any moment. Be warned!"

Sappy trembled and called to Wizen who had been sleeping soundly.

"What is it, young Sappy?" Wizen asked as he gave a big yawn.

"You were right," Sappy said nervously. "The storm is brewing. The jay has seen it."

The bird nodded its head and tail.

Then the sycamore began to tremble. "Look at my leaves." His last remaining leaves were all fluttering, and then his branches began to sway. "It's coming," the sycamore shrieked.

"Brace yourself," said old Wizen. "Try and bend with the wind," the old oak advised Sappy. "We heavier trees are just going to have to stand firm."

The silence was broken by a strange

whining sound. This was followed by a long wailing, then a powerful roar. The storm ripped through the forest with such fury that trees and bushes began to fall and become uprooted.

"It's getting closer! Hang on, dear friends!" Wizen called to the nearby trees.

Leaves blew into the air; branches were torn from the trees. The trees tried to hold fast to the ground, but the wind seemed to get stronger by the minute.

Crash! The great lime tree fell to the ground.

Down came the Corsican pine taking a silver birch with it.

Sappy swayed back and forward, hoping he could withstand the violent winds. Then he heard another loud snap. The sycamore tree was split apart. Poor Sappy became rigid with fear. Then the wind caught him with such fury that it completely uprooted him, sending him too crashing to the forest floor.

The storm cut through the forest like a giant axe, and left destruction everywhere before finally moving over Eagle Mountain.

There was a strange silence after the terrible storm. The sky was grey and there was a chill in the air. A mistle thrush was the first creature to brave an appearance on top of Wizen. With a few encouraging words from the old oak the mistle thrush broke into a beautiful forest song. Its rich melodious piping sounds brought a sense of tranquillity to the storm-damaged forest. Wizen checked his crown. He had lost a few branches here and there, but apart from that he was in good shape. He called out to the other trees to find out how they had fared.

Some, like himself, had branches torn off. Others were sheltered by the larger trees and received only minor injuries. But there were heavy losses. Larch, ash, birch, willow, hazel, chestnut and sycamore were down – some had snapped like twigs. Over a quarter of the forest trees in the path of the storm were knocked or damaged.

Sappy slowly became aware of the warm friendly voice of Wizen calling gently to him.　He had been knocked down and knocked out.

"I'm so sorry, dear boy," said Wizen sadly.

"Oh, don't be sad for me – the only damage I suffered was being uprooted."

"Well, that's a very serious thing for a tree," said Vicky the Holly. "Very serious indeed. Unfortunately we are all so fastened to the forest floor that none of us can move to lend you a helping branch."

A fox padded up a track. "The men are coming. The men are coming!"

The animals and birds went back into hiding.

"Stay very quiet," Wizen warned.

As the men trampled the undergrowth, the loud sound of the chainsaws were heard as they cut into the felled trees. The trees that took years to grow were cut up into logs within hours. Sappy could feel his heart pounding as the men came near. Their gruff voices made him very nervous but he did his best not to tremble.

They stayed all day cutting up the trees, dragging them out of the forest with tractors and chains, then placing the wood onto large trucks. It was a terrible sight for the standing trees to have to witness. They could say or do nothing but watch in sadness while their friends were hauled away. The forest stayed silent for days.

One chilly night Twitch the Tawny Owl roused himself and flew down the forest which was bathed in the moon's silvery light. "They're gone," he hooted solemnly. "The men have finally left the forest." His voice could be heard clearly in the still air. He flew over and alighted on Sappy. "How are you, dear Sappy?" he asked tenderly.

"Oh, quite well, Twitch, thank you. I hope my trunk makes a suitable perch for you."

"Oh, an excellent one," said the owl. "Better than any branch I've ever sat on."

"Oh, I'm so pleased," said Sappy. "You know . . . I've been very dizzy lying like this but now I'm getting rather used to it. It's very interesting looking up at the sky from this viewpoint – at the lovely full moon and its family of stars."

"You're very brave," said Vicky the Holly. "We are all so proud of you."

"Thanks!" said Sappy. "All one can do is try to make the most of it."

Ruddy the Red Fox appeared alongside Sappy. "Sorry to hear you're down!"

"Thank you, Ruddy." Then Sappy noticed a thistle sticking into the side of Ruddy's fur. "That must be sore," he said.

"It is," said Ruddy. "But I just can't manage to shift it."

"Why not rub up against my thin

branches? It might help to dislodge that prickly thing."

"Good idea," said Twitch the Owl.

The fox climbed through Sappy's thin branches and rubbed its side along the twiglets. "That did it." He grinned broadly as the annoying prickly thistle was removed from his fur. Thanking Sappy with a "Take care!" he padded away.

Soon the hedgehog arrived along with some bats. They wished Sappy well and told him they would be going for their long sleep and they hoped somehow he would be made to stand again and grow tall in the forest.

"I'd need a miracle for that, but thanks for your kind words." Sappy wished them all a good sleep and lots of lovely dreams.

Nearly all the birds and animals over the coming weeks came to visit Sappy. He was so popular with the forest folk. The red deer even tried to push him upright with his twelve-pointed antler, but it was useless. He couldn't manage, not even with help from the other deer and Biff, the Badger.

"How are you making out, dear friend?" Wizen asked.

"Well, thank you, but the nights are getting very cold – the forest floor is covered in hoar frost."

"Well, it's Winter's time now," said Wizen, "so we must expect the cold and the frost – it's their time!"

It gave Sappy comfort to see the big strong form of the old oak with his broad branches inking across the azure sky.

Weeks passed and the days became shorter and colder. There had been heavy snow. Wizen kept his young friend amused with wonderful stories of the time when the forest was young, and how men of old built the finest ships that sailed the seven seas with timbers from this forest, and how they built strong houses and splendid cathedrals with the wood, not to mention all the fine furniture and beautiful wooden carvings.

"You can be very proud of being a tree," said Wizen. "We have been a haven and a shelter for so many creatures, even the humans. Not that they appreciate it," he sighed. Then Wizen's tone changed. "You know, tomorrow is called Christmas Day."

"Christmas . . . what's that?" asked Sappy.

"Well, it's a special time," said Wizen. "Strange things can happen at such a time."

"Scary?" asked Sappy.

"No," chuckled Wizen. "But strange nonetheless. My great-grandfather said his family once saw the most beautiful star ever to appear in the sky one Christmas Night. There was the sound of beautiful singing heard from the sky on that special night so long ago . . ."

"Have you ever seen any strange things?" asked Sappy.

"Indeed I have," said Wizen. "One Christmas Eve a very jolly human called Santa Claus stopped by, wearing a suit as red as Vicky's berries. He had a white beard and he rode in a sleigh pulled by twelve reindeer – their leader was called Rudolph and he had a glowing red nose. Santa came to leave presents for a very kind family of humans who lived in the forest back then. Of course, they are long gone, moved to a town or city. But I'll never forget the sight of this friendly old man with his sleigh-bells that rang out a lovely cheerful tune throughout the forest. His deer grazed on the lichen that grows on our branches and trunks. Then as soon as he delivered the presents to the children he and the deer were away over the treetops and across the starry sky."

"Wow!" said Sappy. "That's amazing! Reindeer that can fly! You're so lucky to have seen that."

"Well, yes," said Wizen.

"Have you any more stories about Christmas?"

"Yes," said Wizen. "One night this poor little robin . . ."

"Shush," said Vicky the Holly. "A man has entered the forest."

They all kept deadly quiet, listening to the heavy footfall as the man approached. They watched the shadowy figure move closer. He carried a torch that pierced the darkness, and in the other hand he carried a sack and an axe.

He stopped at Vicky. "What a fine show of berries! I'll take some of those branches." He pulled a pair of shears from the sack and, snipping several branches from the holly tree, he placed them in the sack.

Then he looked down at Sappy lying below him on the forest floor. He stood examining the tree. Then he put down his torch, grabbed his axe with his two hands and raised it over his head. Sappy trembled as he feared the worst. He closed his eyes. Next there was a loud snapping sound. The man thought he heard someone shout. "No!" He looked around but realised it must be only the wind blowing through the trees.

* * *

Sappy awoke and saw a most wonderful sight. He was bathed in beautiful, coloured lights. He wondered if he was dreaming. Small lights twinkled blue, green, yellow, red, pink. Some flashed on and off. There were shiny coloured balls hanging from his branches, and strings of glittery gold and silver wrapped around his body. There were small wooden figures hanging from the outer tips of his branches. Jolly snowmen, children dancing and others skating. There was a Santa Claus carrying a bag of toys and another sitting in his sleigh. As Sappy looked down he could see brightly wrapped parcels tucked underneath his bottom branches.

He was surprised to discover that his roots were gone and he was sitting in a large pot with logs to prevent him from toppling over. How curious, thought Sappy. How strange! I wonder what all this means, he asked himself.

He looked around the room in amazement and recognised many of the things Wizen had described in his stories: furniture, books on shelves and a clock ticking the time on the mantelpiece. There was a lovely warm fire burning brightly. Sappy wasn't afraid of it for there was a fireguard to protect him. It must be the home of the man who took me from the forest, he thought. He could see decorations hanging from the ceilings and colourful balloons. Beside the clock were many cards, showing robins in wintertime and trees like him dressed in bright colours.

"That's it!" he said loudly. "It's Christmas time, just like dear Wizen said!"

Sappy looked up to his crown and placed on the very top branch was a beautiful white star that glowed and twinkled. Then he heard the sound of footsteps and the door began to open slowly. Sappy trembled, fearing it was the man again with an axe, or worse – a chainsaw. Two heads peeped around the corner.

"Wow!" said the little boy.

"It's beautiful," said his younger sister.

They slowly entered the room.

"See! Dad did get a tree like he said he would," the boy said brightly.

"It's the nicest Christmas tree I've ever seen," said the girl.

Slowly they moved to the tree, first checking that neither their dad nor mum were about, as they should have been asleep ages ago. Mummy had said that Santa didn't bring presents to children who stayed awake. The little girl reached out and touched one of the twinkling lights.

"Hello," said Sappy.

"Who said that?" said the boy, startled.

"It wasn't me," said the girl. "Honest."

They looked about the room but there was no one else there. Only them.

"I'm Sappy! What are your names?"

"The tree said it!" exclaimed the little girl.

Sappy began to chuckle and some of the small bells on his branches started to chime.

"You can talk," said the little girl in amazement.

"Of course," said Sappy.

"I'm Sarah," said the little girl.

"You can shake one of my branches, but not too hard," Sappy said brightly.

The little girl gripped a branch and shook it gently.

"And you, young fella, what's your name?"

"Aindriú ," he said. "You're the best tree we've ever had . . . a talking Christmas tree!"

"Oh, so that's what I am! A Christmas tree! I used to be a conifer tree and now I'm a Christmas tree. How exciting! That's why I'm dressed up so fancy!"

The children giggled.

"Wizen told me a little about Christmas, but he would be amazed to see me now all dressed up like this. A real Christmas tree!"

"Who is Wizen?" asked Aindriú .

Sappy explained that he was an old oak tree, and that he was his best friend. He also explained how a big storm had blown him down along with many other dear friends. "I'm very lucky. I think I'm the only one who has ended up as a Christmas tree."

"You must be sad not being with your friends in the forest," said Sarah.

"Well, I do miss them, to tell you the truth, but I'm also delighted to be here with you two special people."

"We're so pleased to have you in our home," said the boy.

Sarah looked sad.

"What's the matter?" Sappy asked.

"There are lots of lovely presents for us

under the tree and soon Santa will come with a special surprise present for us as well. But there's no present for you."

"Maybe Santa will bring you one," said Aindriú brightly.

"If he doesn't, you can have one of ours," said Sarah.

"Well, that's very kind of you," said Sappy, "but I've received a very special present already."

"You have?" said Aindriú .

"What is it?" asked Sarah.

"It's the gift of friendship from you. And that's the best present anyone could get."

Suddenly there was a noise of a door opening. "It's Santa!" said Aindriú . "No, it's Dad!"

Their father popped his head around the door. "I thought I heard some noise down here."

"We were just talking to – I mean looking at the lovely tree. It's beautiful," said Sarah. "It's my favourite tree in the whole wide world," said her brother.

Her father grinned. "Is that so?"

They both nodded.

"Listen you two, it's very late. You better get back to bed before Santa arrives."

Then they heard the front door open.

"It's Santa!" said Sarah.

"No, it's Mum," said Aindriú .

They went out into the hall.

"Why are you two still up?" she said, pretending to be cross.

"We were looking at our lovely Christmas tree."

"Well, I'd better take a look." They went into the sitting-room. "Well, isn't that just lovely!" she exclaimed. "And beautifully decorated."

Their dad looked very pleased with himself. "Well, I think it's time we all went to bed. Tomorrow is a very special day and we'll be having lots of guests arriving for Christmas dinner."

"Goodnight, Sappy," said Aindriú .

"Who?" asked his father.

"That's the tree's name," said Sarah. "Sappy, and he was first told about Christmas by his friend Wizen the Old Oak Tree, who lives in the forest."

"Indeed!" said their dad.

They all went up to bed.

Pamela laughed to herself. "Where do they get their imagination from? Sappy and his friend Wizen the Old Oak Tree, who lives in the forest."

"Well, I'll tell you a strange thing," said Harry. "Where I got that tree in the forest there was a large oak tree close by, and when I chopped down the tree I thought I heard voices."

It was just after midnight and things had become very quiet. Sappy was just about to sleep when he heard the sound of sleigh-bells outside the window. He looked out and there was Santa Claus. He was giving his deer the carrots that the children had left out for them. Then like magic Santa was in the room placing presents for the family under the tree. Sappy was so astonished and excited he didn't say a word.

"What a beautiful tree!" declared Santa as he warmed himself by the fire. Then he noticed that there was a cup of tea and some mince pies on the mantelpiece with a Christmas card made by the children for him. "How very thoughtful," said Santa as he drank down the tea and ate the mince pies. "Well, time to go," he said to himself. "I've still a very busy night ahead of me. A merry Christmas to all who reside here!" He smiled broadly. "Ho! Ho! Ho!" Then just like magic he was away into his sleigh and heading over the rooftops. One of the reindeer had a glowing red nose.

Sappy was very excited to have seen Santa Claus. He was just like old Wizen had described him, a large, round, jolly man with a big white beard and a broad friendly smile. He wore a red suit trimmed with white and carried a sack full of presents.

Oh, how happy Sappy would be if he could talk to old Wizen just once more and tell him about his Christmas! But sadly that was not to be.

Sappy looked out the window and saw a very bright star twinkling in the sky. That must be one of those wishing stars that the old oak had spoken of. Sappy made a wish. He wished that all his friends in the forest were safe and well on this very special night. Then to his amazement a shaft of blue-white light shone down through the window onto him, giving him a very beautiful feeling, and making him feel tingly all over. Then slowly the light withdrew. Sappy fell into a beautiful deep sleep.

Next morning when he awoke he found Sarah and Aindriú playing beside him with the toys Santa had left for them.

"Good morning," said Sappy.

"You really can talk!" Sarah exclaimed. "I thought I only dreamed it!"

"Do you like our Christmas toys?" Aindriú asked.

"They look like fun," Sappy remarked. "I was still awake when Santa arrived."

"You were?" said Aindriú excitedly.

"Yes," said Sappy proudly. "He thought I looked very smart, dressed up like this. He ate the mince pies and drank the tea. And he gave the carrots to his reindeer. They were delighted. Oh, by the way, it's true that Rudolph has a red nose. I saw it glow as they flew into the sky," Sappy added.

* * *

In the afternoon the guests arrived at the house and they all agreed that it was a splendid-looking Christmas tree. Sappy was very pleased. He wanted to say thanks but he thought he'd better not talk to the grown-ups . . . they might think him strange.

He stood there in the corner with his lights twinkling while everyone enjoyed their Christmas dinner. Later on they pulled crackers and the guests sang carols and recited some seasonal verse.

A marvellous Christmas was had by all and especially by Sappy who was discovering Christmas for the first time.

Well, weeks passed and it was time to take down the Christmas decorations and remove all the lights from the Christmas tree, and put them away until next year.

Sappy didn't know what was happening. He thought that Christmas might last all year round.

"What's going to happen to our tree?" asked Sarah and Aindriú anxiously.

"We'll recycle it," said their dad, "so it will be put to a good use."

"No, please! Not this tree!" said the children. "Please, Dad! No!"

"Whatever is the matter, children?" asked their mother.

"This tree is special," said Aindriú .

"All trees are special, dear," his mother retorted.

"Look at this," said their father in amazement as he pulled the tree from the pot.

"What is it?" asked Pamela.

"How amazing! The tree has grown new roots!"

The children jumped up and down and cheered excitedly.

"Sappy got a Christmas present after all," they cried with great joy.

"I've never seen anything like it," said their puzzled father.

"Please, Daddy, let's bring it back to the

forest and plant it where you found it," Sarah pleaded.

"That's a wonderful idea," said their mother.

"Why ever not?" said their dad, smiling.

"Wrap up well and put on your boots," their mother insisted, "and we'll go right away."

They drove to the outskirts of the forest, parked the car and walked into the trees carrying Sappy. Pamela and Harry thought they could hear whispering but it must just be the wind in the branches.

"There's the place," their dad said proudly. "I couldn't forget that old oak tree there. It's got such character!"

And they carefully planted Sappy beside the oak tree.

"There! As good as new," said their father as he pressed down the earth around the tree roots. "Happy?" he asked.

The children nodded.

"Goodbye, Sappy," said Aindriú .

"Thank you for being our best ever Christmas tree," said Sarah. Their mum and dad laughed loudly.

"Well, that's better than recycling," said their father as they headed back to the car.

Voices echoed around the forest . . . "Sappy's back – Sappy's returned!"

All the forest folk came out to witness this event.

"It's a miracle," said old Wizen trying to hold back the tears of joy.

"Hi, everyone," said Sappy. "Did you miss me? I'm so glad to be back."

The birds were so pleased that they all broke into song. When they had finished Sappy said proudly. "Listen everyone! I've a story to tell! It's about a tree that discovered Christmas."

The End

The
Christmas Gift

The sun hung like a lantern, low in the sky. Hungry songbirds flitted along the hedgerows to feed on the last of the autumn's bounty of berries. Winter had gripped the land. Blankets of snow lay across fields, building up near walls and hedges. The mallards waddled on the frozen lakes. Visiting whooper swans called overhead as they headed for the estuary. Among the bare branches of a rowan tree

47

sat a male robin. He sang briefly before flying to the warm comfort of the old stable. There he settled down in the corner where old swallows' saucer-nests remained, reminding him of warm summer days long gone, along with the swallows.

Outside, as dusk painted her delicate colours across the sky, Conor finished his snowman. His dog Bran barked for attention and pulled at his clothes.

"What do you think?" asked Conor.

The dog barked again.

"Good, I'm glad you like it," said Conor proudly.

Up the narrow road Conor's father walked, pulling large branches and faggots on a sled. Conor and Bran hurried to greet him.

"What do you think of my snowman, Father?" said Conor, pointing.

"Very good," said his father. Then he added, "It's a pity we cannot bring it to life. We could do with a bit of extra help around here." He sighed as he removed the rope from his shoulders that he used to pull the heavy wood along. "Well, we've enough fuel for the next week or so." He smiled at his eight-year-old son. "Tell me, son, did you melt down some snow for water?"

"I did, Father. It's already inside."

His father pulled off his cap and tossed Conor's hair. "You're a good boy. Now it's time to go inside. Supper will be ready soon." He looked to the mountains knowing the chilling winds were gathering. He hoped his sheep were okay. He hadn't been able to get up to check on them for several days.

Inside their hut of mud and wattles sat his wife Gráinne. She was weaving a small blanket.

"Good evening, dear," said Kevin. "Another cold night ahead." He sighed.

"It's to be expected this time of year. Sit down and have some warm broth and bread."

He looked at the tiny blanket.

"Nearly finished," she smiled.

"And it looks lovely. What a splendid pattern! You are clever!"

"I hope it will be warm enough," she said anxiously. She got up to get the supper.

"Stay where you are, Gráinne. We're well able to look after ourselves." He winked at Conor.

They sat down and tucked into their food. "Mmm . . ." Kevin sighed. "This food chases the chill out of my old bones."

"Old bones at twenty-nine?" retorted Gráinne.

"After cutting up that windblown tree

and dragging it over a mile I feel about seventy-five."

She got up and massaged his shoulders.

"Ahh! That feels good," said Kevin. "You've got the touch."

Conor fed some scraps to Bran who was sitting beside his wooden stool. "Well, now that the winter solstice is past let us hope the weather will begin to improve," said Kevin. "Gráinne, dear, I'd better go and check on the sheep tonight. I don't want to lose them to this weather or those hungry wolves."

"Not tonight," said Gráinne.

"But I must," Kevin insisted. "Otherwise we'll lose the lot of them."

Gráinne cupped Kevin's face in her hand. "I think tonight is my night. I've had the feeling all day."

Conor studied his parents; they both

looked so anxious. His father paced around and scratched at his red beard.

"I'll watch over the sheep," Conor offered.

"Nonsense," said his father. "You're too young. If only my brother were here!"

"Please, Father," said Conor. "You promised you would take me some night when I'm older."

"Well, you're only eight," snapped Kevin.

"I'll be nine in springtime when the flower is on the hawthorn. I'll wrap up well and take Bran with me."

"What do you think, Gráinne?" Kevin asked.

Gráinne looked at Conor. "Do you really think you can find your way up to the hills and back again?"

Conor smiled and nodded. "With Bran's help."

His father sighed. "Very well. Wrap up well. Take some food. Take my staff."

They both hugged Conor. "You're a brave little boy," said his father.

"You be careful!" his mother said, pointing her finger. "Take the sheepskin cloak. When you're up on the hills find a sheltered spot under a boulder and tuck yourself in. And keep the dog close to you. That way you'll both stay warm."

His father handed him a lighted torch made of hazel branches and rags smeared with grease and tar. "This should light your way, son. If you can manage, try and make a small fire for yourself up on the hills. I have left small bundles of faggots at different spots, marked by some small stones stacked upon one another. At any sign of danger from wolves or wild boar just wave your lighted torch at them."

Conor set off with his staff, and the torch to light his way. Bran ran a few feet ahead.

He looked back once at the farm. His parents stood in the doorway waving goodbye to him.

The wind had picked up and was moaning through the trees. Conor felt a mixture of excitement and fear. He had never been out so late before, especially on his own. He could see his breath like smoke as he moved up the narrow pathway. Dark clouds gathered overhead and a light snow began to fall.

He watched as the snowflakes danced down from the sky. He opened his mouth and tried to catch some. "You try!" he called to Bran. The dog just hurried back to him and wagged its tail. By now he was up quite high in the hills, but still saw no sign of their sheep. He looked back over the valley. The snow made the night seem brighter. All was shrouded in silence. The only light he could see was from their farm. The small yellow light that came from the house looked like a fallen star.

After a time the snow stopped and the strong winds died down. The night sky became clear again and stars shone out. Conor imagined he could just reach up and touch one. He walked along a steep ridge. Bran barked. Sheep bleated.

Conor could barely make out the sheep against the snow. He was so grateful for Bran who seemed to have no trouble seeing in the dark and rounding up the sheep into a tight flock.

"Good doggie," said Conor.

He searched until he located one of the stone markings made by his father, and there he found a bundle of small twigs hidden under some heather.

He found a dug-out in the hill which his father used and old traces of a fire inside small circular stones. He lit a small fire, a skill he had learned from his father, and settled down for his long night vigil. Bran licked his face and sat beside him. Conor produced the small amount of food he had and shared it with the dog. He was sorry he

had nothing to give to the sheep. They must be very hungry, he thought. It was very difficult for them to forage for food under the heavy blanket of snow.

As the night wore on Conor began to shiver from the cold. He teeth chattered. He pulled the sheepskin cloak more tightly around him and hugged the dog. Something moved beyond the light of the fire. Conor grabbed hold of the torch and waved it out in front of them.

A mountain hare sat bolt upright, then darted into the darkness. "It's only a hare." He heaved a sigh of relief.

The light of the torch began to fade; soon it would be spent. Still the fire was giving off a bright and warm flame. Tiredness overcame him and he began to doze. Bran snuggled closer.

Then a loud, bloodcurdling shriek

pierced the night. Conor was jolted out of his sleep by the weird noise. What was it? he wondered. He could feel the hair rising on the back of his neck. Directly overhead, like a phantom, a barn owl glided past. "It's an owl," he said, relieved. "It's probably hungry too." He brushed Bran's fur. "We've nothing to fear from it." Then as quickly as the owl appeared it vanished in the still night.

Conor had just settled back down to sleep when a sound far more eerie filled the night. It was a pack of wolves. They were howling. Conor trembled, hoping they wouldn't come near him. Their mournful wails seemed to get louder and sound closer. Conor grabbed up the staff and held it tightly. He became fearful as the fire began to fade. There were no more sticks to place on the embers.

He could hear the sheep making distress sounds. They were all too aware that the hungry wolves were near. Conor sat like a frightened rabbit, his body shaking with fear. Bran licked his face. Suddenly the wolves became quiet and light flooded the hillside.

Conor looked around in wonder, and then noticed a star in the sky that seemed to be

much brighter than the rest. As he watched it, it seemed to grow in size and twinkle even more brightly.

"Look," he pointed excitedly. "Can you see?"

The star hovered overhead. Its light seemed brighter than a full moon. They were now bathed in starlight as it passed over; he felt a great sense of calm and peace. All his fear had vanished.

Then, to his amazement, he began to hear voices. Beautiful singing echoed across the night sky.

"Listen," said Conor. "The stars are singing." The dog sat looking skywards, its ears erect, its tail wagging.

As they watched, pulsating light poured from the bright star. Soon the sky was curtained by rainbow shapes. The light seemed to move with the music and spill overhead in waves of colour. Conor was so busy watching the amazing event that he failed to notice a stranger standing alongside, but gradually became aware of a presence. He looked around and there stood a tall man dressed in long robes of white.

"Do not be afraid, Conor," said the man. His voice was warm and friendly. "May I join you?"

Conor nodded. The man sat down beside him. Bran was resting across Conor's feet.

"You're a brave little boy sitting up here all on your own," said the stranger.

Conor explained why he was there.

"The sheep are safe," said the man.

Conor looked towards the flock. They were busy grazing on a bright patch of green. He rubbed his eyes and looked again. They were in what looked like a lush summer field. The man smiled and stretched his hands over the spent fire and soon it was burning as brightly as ever.

"Wow, how did you do that?" asked Conor.

The man just smiled.

Conor looked at the handsome man with long golden hair and eyes that glowed pale blue in the firelight. "How come you know my name?" asked Conor. "I don't know yours."

The man extended his hand in friendship. "I'm Gabriel." They shook hands. "I was just passing when I picked up your mother's thoughts. This is a very special time. It's a time when heaven meets earth."

Conor did not understand what he meant, but was glad of the stranger's company.

"Where are you going to?" Conor asked.

"A distant land where a special baby is to be born."

"I hope it's warmer than here," said Conor.

Gabriel smiled. "Young Conor, tell me what your favourite food is."

"Well, I love the wild-berry pie my mother makes for us when the berries grow on the hedgerows."

"And your favourite drink?"

"I love milk, but sometimes Mother can make a warm fruit drink. That's delicious."

"Close your eyes," said Gabriel, "and count to five."

Conor did as he was told. An instant later he opened them to discover he had warm blackberry tart in one hand and a fruit drink in the other.

"That's amazing," said Conor. "How do you do that magic?"

"It's a secret." Gabriel winked at Conor.

Conor tucked into the food. The man just watched and smiled. Then two other men appeared nearby. They looked just as beautiful as Gabriel, Conor thought as he watched them.

"Well, young Conor," said Gabriel, "I must be going . . . my friends Michael and Uriel are waiting for me. It's been very nice talking to you."

Conor shook his hand again. "Thank you, sir, for the food and the fire."

"You have a good rest," said Gabriel. "And don't worry about anything. The sheep will be safe and you will find a green pathway down the hills to your home in the morning. Follow that and you won't go wrong." He touched Conor on the shoulder. "There is a special surprise awaiting you when you go home. I want you to give this to your parents. Tell them it's a Christmas gift." He produced a beautiful woollen blanket with star designs on it. Then a white object. "This is a candle. Light the top here and it will bring light to your home."

"Thank you," said Conor. "You are very kind."

The man said goodbye and walked towards the other men.

Conor noticed that he left no footprints in the snow. The air was filled with the fragrance of wild flowers. Conor suddenly felt very sleepy and lay back on the blanket. He fell into a deep sleep.

Early next morning he found that bread and food had been left for him and the dog. He quickly ate it and hurried home, following the new pathway Gabriel had told him about.

When he arrived home he was surprised to hear crying from inside the hut. He hurried inside and there were his parents, and to his amazement his mother was holding a beautiful baby in her arms.

"Thank heavens, you're safe, son," cried his mother.

"Look, Conor," smiled his father. "You have a sister."

Conor couldn't believe his eyes. "What's her name?" he asked brightly. "Emer," said his mother.

"Conor! Where did you get that beautiful cloth?" his father enquired.

"It's a star blanket! It's a present from a man named Gabriel who I met in the mountains. He told me to tell you it's a Christmas gift."

The End

Uncle Fred's Special Christmas

Fred Hardy had just finished writing his Christmas cards. He gave a big yawn and stretched. It was getting near his bedtime. He would post the cards first thing in the morning. Have breakfast in one of the big stores. Perhaps take a walk in Central Park and feed the birds.

He looked around the room. It was full of toys, although Fred had no family and lived on his own. Every year he bought toys for the children in the poorer neighbourhoods. He would wrap them up carefully and deliver them on Christmas Eve to the different families. The parents were always very appreciative of this old man's kindness

towards their children. Sometimes he'd meet the children after Christmas and they would show him the wonderful toys they got from Santa Claus.

"Oh you must have been very good to get a second present from Father Christmas," he would say to them.

Although Fred was known and loved by everyone in the neighbourhood, no one knew exactly where he lived. Or that he always spent Christmas on his own. It was not that he wasn't invited to people's homes. He was, but he always declined.

If ever a man loved Christmas, it was Fred Hardy. He loved to hear the carols being sung by the children, to see the city dressed with decorations and colourful twinkling lights. Fred lived in a high-rise apartment block in one of the poorer areas of New York.

Before bedtime Fred would switch off the lights in his apartment and stare out the window. That was one good thing about where he lived. He had a wonderful view out over the city and it always looked so beautiful by night.

Time for bed, he told himself.

He was about to head for his bedroom, as he did at the same time every evening, when he heard a faint tap at the kitchen window. The sound was like that of a bird hitting off the glass. Sometimes the pigeons accidentally flew at the window and were stunned. Fred would put them in a box until they recovered. He would feed them and release them later.

As he got closer to the window, he was amazed to see the window seemed to be coated with strange rainbow light. How very strange, he thought, as the glass glistened blue, pink and yellow. Then he heard a voice say, "Silly me! I'm always doing that."

"Who said that?" he asked, looking around.

"Me! That's who!"

Fred looked down at a tiny fairy-like creature outside the window. "Aren't you going to let me in?" she demanded.

Fred rubbed his eyes and put on his glasses. The little creature was still there. He opened the window and the fairy flew in leaving a trail of light that soon vanished like a puff of smoke. Fred watched the fairy fly in circles around the apartment and the trails of light that emanated from her looked truly beautiful in the darkened room.

"Am I dreaming?" he blurted out.

"Are you asleep?" said the fairy.

"No," said Fred, "I don't think so."

"Then you're not dreaming, silly!" she laughed. "Perhaps you'd better sit down and I'll explain the reason for my visit."

Fred sat as the beautiful creature flew over and alighted on his shoulder. "I'm Snowdrop the Fairy and I've come to ask you for your help. It's not for me but for someone very important."

"Well, if I can be of any assistance – "

"You can," she interrupted. "That's why I've come."

"Well, if you don't mind me asking, where did you come from and who needs help?" he enquired.

"Oh, now I'm the silly one! I should have explained earlier. I've flown here all the way from the North Pole, and that is far, believe me, even with fairy magic."

"The North Pole!" said Fred in amazement.

"You *have* heard of the North Pole?"
Fred nodded.

"Where the polar bears live," she added.
"Not the penguins – they live at the South
Pole."

"You want me to help polar bears?"
asked Fred.

The fairy burst into laughter and flew
around the room making a complete circle
of light. "No, no, no," she laughed even
louder. "To help Father Christmas. Kris
Kindle. Santa Claus. You must have heard
of HIM!" She landed on his other shoulder.

"Of course. Everyone has," said Fred.

"Then you will help?"

"Help Santa? Yes. Of course! If I can,
certainly!"

"There's no time to lose. It's only a week
to Christmas Eve and there is lots to be
done, so much to be arranged. It's our

busiest time of the year. The pixies, elves and fairies are working around the clock."

"Pardon me for interrupting," said Fred. "What's wrong with Santa Claus?"

"He's down with terrible flu," she sighed. "The first he has had in years. He's sneezing and coughing, and he's feeling very poorly indeed."

"Well, I have some things that might help," said Fred brightly. He went to the kitchen got some vitamin C, honey and lemon, and Echinacea drops. "Give these to dear ole Santa. They should help him."

"You must come to the North Pole."

"The North Pole? Me?" said Fred.

"You do want to help poor Santa?" asked Snowdrop.

"Of course, anything for Santa Claus but how?"

"Leave the how to me!" She folded her

arms and looked him up and down. "Those clothes will never do." She waved a tiny wand over Fred. "There, that's better." She smiled.

Fred stood there amazed, for he was now wearing warm outdoor clothes and snow boots.

"I don't suppose you can fly? No, I guess not," said the fairy.

"I'll phone the airport first thing in the morning," said Fred. "They might get me a flight somewhere close to the North Pole."

Snowdrop looked around the room and picked up a pencil. "Mmmm, I could make it big."

"Whatever you are thinking, young lady, forget it! I like something solid under me when flying."

"I could make you small like me," she suggested.

"Thank you very much, but no thanks," said Fred.

Snowdrop flew into the kitchen and then she gave out a loud cheer. "This will do! Perfect."

Uncle Fred went in to see what she had found. Next minute a piece of his favourite china, a saucer, flew past him out the window. Fred looked after it. He couldn't believe his eyes. The minute it was outside the saucer became larger and hovered just below the window ledge.

"Wait a minute," said Fred. "I hope you don't expect me to fly to the North Pole on that saucer."

The fairy smiled and nodded.

"No way," said Fred. "I'm too old for that kind of thing. I'll just try phoning the airport now . . ." But before he knew it the fairy had used her magic on him and he found himself sitting in the hovering saucer.

The fairy joined him. "All set?" she asked.

"Yes, I think so," said Fred nervously.

Next moment they were shooting over the Manhattan skyline. Fred held tightly to the sides of the saucer, afraid to look down. Then, after a few minutes, he opened one eye. They were flying over the Empire State Building. The city looked very beautiful. He began to relax.

"Let's fly under the bridge," said the fairy.

They circled in and around the skyscrapers, then flew under the Brooklyn Bridge. Fred began to enjoy himself. It reminded him of his childhood, when the carnival came to town, only this was like no roller-coaster ride he'd ever been on.

They circled about, zigzagging in and around New York, then they headed out across the dark sky.

There were many reports to radio stations that night of people seeing a flying saucer over the city. As they left New York behind them, the sky became clear, studded with stars. Uncle Fred had never seen it so beautiful as this before. They flew low over the sea, passing the occasional sea vessel. Uncle Fred even got a glimpse of a great whale moving on the surface of the dark waters, which was a real treat.

The fairy began to jump up and down. "We're nearly there," she shouted in excited tones.

Uncle Fred looked to the distance. He could see curtains of light across the sky. "The Aurora Borealis," he pointed excitedly.

As they approached the ice kingdom they passed over strangely shaped icebergs, then across a land locked in snow, frost and ice. Uncle Fred could see no sign of houses or anything resembling a dwelling place. Then he noticed a large mountain up ahead. It was shaped like an ear. "That's it," said Snowdrop. "Ear Mountain."

They circled around it then flew into the entrance at the hole of the ear. As they slowly journeyed inside the mountain, Uncle Fred could not believe his eyes. The walls on either side sparkled with beautiful crystals and precious stones.

"Not much farther now," said the fairy, as the tunnel widened into a large opening inside the mountain. There, a charming village was built around a large colourful castle. All kinds of beautiful lights streamed through the air. These, Uncle Fred knew, were the fairies. Below, elves, pixies, gnomes and little people were busy going about their business.

"Hello, everybody!" shouted Snowdrop brightly.

But no one seemed to take any notice. They were all so preoccupied with getting ready for Christmas.

Snowdrop pulled out her wand and wrote in big letters of light over the village:

Uncle Fred has arrived!

Everything and everyone came to a standstill, some even bumping into one another. They looked at the man sitting on the saucer. Uncle Fred smiled back nervously. Then they all broke out into loud cheering and applauding.

"See!" said Snowdrop. "They're delighted you're here."

A snowy owl flew towards him, and on its back sat the Queen of the Fairies. Fred had thought Snowdrop was beautiful, but the queen was even more radiant – she had golden hair and rainbow light emanated from her as she moved.

"You are most welcome to the North Pole, our crystal kingdom. And, of course, the home of Father Christmas and his families."

"Delighted to be here, and to make your acquaintance," said Uncle Fred.

"You are very kind to come at such short notice." She touched him with her wand.

Uncle Fred floated gently down from the saucer.

"Follow me," she said warmly.

Fred turned and thanked Snowdrop for a most exciting trip. "You're welcome!" she smiled. They headed inside the great castle. Fred could see all the pixies, elves, gnomes and little folk standing to attention. They all cheered again and applauded loudly as he entered.

"Come and sit by the fire, and warm yourself after your long journey."

"Well, that's very kind of you." Uncle Fred removed his overcoat, hat and boots. He looked towards Snowdrop.

"Oh, don't worry about me," she responded, as if she could read his mind. "We fairies don't feel the cold."

Elves entered from the kitchen with a warm supper and a mug of hot chocolate for him.

"You relax and enjoy that," said the queen. "And have a good night's rest. Tomorrow I will let you have an audience with Father Christmas – if he's up to it. The guest bedroom is prepared for you, when you finish your supper," said the queen.

Uncle Fred slept like a log in his wooden bed and had the most wonderful dreams.

The next morning he awoke feeling very refreshed. After breakfast he was shown the workshop where the talented little folk made all the wonderful toys. Some specialised in making presents like music boxes and musical instruments; others were busy making soft toys. Some could be seen painting small metal cars, trains, boats and aeroplanes.

Santa's helpers took great pride in making the toys for they knew how important these gifts were to the children on Christmas morning.

There was even an area where old toys were restored to their former glory. The fairies, using their magic did a great deal of this work. Some of the fairies specialised in delicate gifts like snow domes and glass figurines. Uncle Fred marvelled at all the wonderful gifts. He felt like a young boy again in such a magical place.

There were so many areas to see in the toy factory. He entered through a chocolate door and sampled some of the wonderful sweets, chocolates, and candy. There were Selection Boxes, chocolate Santas and marshmallow snowmen piled high. Other areas made balloons, jigsaw puzzles, games and electronic gifts.

After his lengthy tour around the workshops, he visited the post-room where all the letters for Santa arrived. The letters were all arranged in special compartments starting with the country of origin, then counties or states, cities, towns, villages etc, the age groups, whether they were boys or girls, toddlers or babies. Uncle

Fred wondered how they could keep track of them all, but they managed somehow with a little magic from the fairies.

Uncle Fred asked why the crystal mountain was shaped like an ear.

"Why do you have ears?" the Head Sorter retorted.

"Well, to listen with," said Uncle Fred.

"Same with Ear Mountain. We can hear whether children are being good or bold – if they are kind and helpful, or mean and cruel."

"I see," said Uncle Fred. "How very interesting."

"We don't like to hear about bad behaviour, especially any kind of bullying, or being cruel to animals."

"I agree," said Uncle Fred. Then he felt a light tap on his shoulder. He turned and there was the Fairy Queen.

"Father Christmas will see you now."

Fred felt a surge of excitement at the thought of seeing the great man himself. They climbed the stairs to the top of the castle. They could hear loud sneezing and coughing as they walked along a corridor. The Fairy Queen tapped on the bedroom door.

"Come in," said a jolly but hoarse voice.

They entered. Uncle Fred looked over at the large bed. And there lay a big, rotund man, with a long white curly beard.

"Welcome," said Santa brightly. "Sorry I couldn't meet you last evening, but I was feeling rather poorly." He blew his nose with a large red handkerchief.

Uncle Fred moved closer to greet him. He could see Santa had a bright red nose from all the blowing.

"My nose looks a bit like Rudolph's, don't you think?" Santa laughed. Then he broke into coughing.

"He won't let us use magic on him," sighed the queen. "Thinks it would be wasteful to use our precious magic to make him better." She whispered, "We don't like to go against his wishes but he can be stubborn at times."

"Leave it to me. I might have a little magic of my own to try. Would you excuse me a moment?" said Fred. He returned with a honey and lemon drink, fortified with vitamin C, and Echinacea drops. "Now, Santa, I insist you drink this up."

"Well, if you say so. But I'm not fond of taking medicine."

"It will do you good," said Fred.

Santa finished the drink. "Mmmm . . . not bad at all," Santa winked. "You're a great fellow to agree to stand in for me on Christmas Eve."

"Well, I'm most happy to help," said Fred. "But I don't think I'm worthy of this great honour."

"Of course you are," said Santa. "We ran a checklist on our North Pole computer. There were a number of very good candidates so we had a vote on it, and you topped the poll."

Uncle Fred felt a little embarrassed. "I really don't know what to say."

"You don't have to say anything. And don't worry – we'll do everything. The reindeer know all the best routes. The fairies and elves will be there to help." Santa looked at him. "We need to get you a red suit and pad you out a bit."

"But it doesn't seem right, me pretending to be you," said Fred.

"You're not pretending to be me – you're my assistant and you're supervising the deliveries of the toys on Christmas Eve."

Fred rubbed his chin.

"We can't disappoint the children," insisted Santa. "That's the number one priority."

"You're right," said Fred. "I'll do it! For the sake of the children and to help you."

"Good man," said Santa.

Uncle Fred was brought out to the warm stables where the reindeer were feeding. The queen introduced Fred to each deer. This is Dasher, Dancer, Prancer, Vixen, Comet, Cupid, Donder, Blitzen . . . and, of course, Rudolph, the red-nosed Reindeer."

Rudolph licked Uncle Fred's hand. The others all nuzzled him.

"I should have brought some carrots," said Fred. "I bought some yesterday."

With that the queen worked her magic, and produced a bucketful of carrots. Fred had fun feeding the carrots to the deer.

"They all like you," said the queen. "Now come and try on some suits to see which one you'd prefer."

Fred did enjoy trying on the different Santa Claus suits. They were all too big, of course, since Uncle Fred was a somewhat slim man. But with a little magic from the fairy queen and some padding, Fred looked rather good. He decided not to use a beard. If any child did see him he would simply say he was Santa's helper.

Later, Uncle Fred was having lunch with the queen and all the elves, fairies, pixies, gnomes and little people. He was sitting at the head of the table and he decided to ask a question. He asked how could all those presents be delivered to all the children in the world in the one night. All the little people stopped and stared at him. There was a deadly silence.

"Was it something I said?" he asked nervously.

The queen smiled. "No, dear Uncle Fred. It's just that we normally don't tell our little secrets – how we achieve things – to any human. But you are a special case," she smiled. "The way we do all those special deliveries in one night is this: we expand time."

"Expand time!" said Uncle Fred. "That's a new one on me."

"It's like being able to stretch out a day, like the way you can stretch a rubber band. The day is still twenty-four hours but each second is expanded. Then, since the day is stretched out, we can work in between that time."

Uncle Fred looked totally confused. "Well, as long as it works, that's the main thing," he quipped.

The queen smiled. All the little folk laughed loudly and the gnomes sitting next to Fred patted him on the back

Christmas Eve finally arrived. Uncle Fred got up bright and early, had his breakfast and got into his Santa Claus suit. He checked that the sleigh was ready and the toys were all in the sacks, which were coded and numbered. And, finally, he checked the lists so he could match the presents to the girl or boy. There could be no mistakes.

"I do love the children who ask for a surprise," said the elf who was in charge of the packing.

"It sure makes things easier all round," said another.

Then, one of the pixies came hurrying up to Uncle Fred as he was about to give some extra carrots to the reindeer. "Come quickly to the castle! It's very important!"

Uncle Fred had no idea what was up. He was sure he'd remembered everything. He'd checked the list three times. He hurried after the pixie.

Inside the castle the pixies, elves, gnomes, little people and fairies all stood around staring at him.

"Is something the matter?" he asked. No one replied. "Well, I admit I don't look anything like Santa even though I've stuffed a pillow down my jacket. But hopefully none of the children will see me."

"It's not that," said the queen softly. "You've done everything so well, helping prepare things so efficiently, even down to taking care of Father Christmas so wonderfully."

"What is it then?" he wondered. "Shouldn't I be on my way?"

"The thing is your medicine worked so well that Father Christmas is completely well again and he won't have to miss a Christmas Eve after all. He's getting ready right now."

"So – I'm afraid we won't be needing your services," said the Chief Gnome awkwardly.

"Oh, I see," said Fred quietly. He was very happy that Santa Claus was well again, but a little disappointed that he wasn't going to make the special trip on the sleigh with the reindeers. "I even practised my 'Ho Ho Ho'," he said sadly.

"We are so sorry," said the queen. She gave him a gift. "This is for you, but you're not to open it until Christmas morning. Snowdrop will bring you safely home."

She flew up and kissed him on the cheek. A tear escaped from his eye. "Thank you all. It's been great fun being with you over the last couple of days. I now understand what you mean about expanding time. It's been the happiest few days of my life. I won't forget your kindness."

There was a loud burst of 'Ho Ho Ho' as Santa came down the stairs, laughing loudly. "I feel as fit as a fiddle and it's all thanks to you, Uncle Fred." He gave him a big hug, then looked around. "Why all the glum faces on Christmas Eve? Cheer up everyone! You've all done a marvellous job as usual. We can be proud that the children of the world will have another special Christmas."

"I was just telling Uncle Fred you were well again and that we didn't need him to ride the sleigh tonight," said the Chief Gnome.

Santa looked at Fred, eyes twinkling. "No, he's not needed to ride the sleigh but I sure hope he'll come and keep me company tonight!"

Uncle Fred's eyes widened. "You'd like me to join you in the sleigh?"

"Of course! Unless you want to go home by saucer," Santa chuckled.

They all laughed and cheered. Then everyone broke into song, the bells rang in the village and the fairies flew about, making the most exquisite colour designs over their heads. Snowdrop wrote, in bright yellow letters in the air:

A VERY HAPPY CHRISTMAS!

Santa climbed into the sleigh. "All aboard?" Uncle Fred sat beside him, with some fairies and elves. "Merry Christmas!" shouted Santa Claus, "To one and all!" The little folk cheered and clapped.

Rudolph guided the sleigh up the crystal tunnel and out across the starry sky. It was Uncle Fred's best Christmas ever.

And Santa Claus admitted he couldn't remember a happier Christmas night.

103